Roobarb

The birds

Poodle Princess

Roobarb & Custard™

Meet the gang!

Mole

Custard

Mouse

Moggy Malone

When Roobarb's trousers flew

www.roobarbandcustard.tv © 1974-2009 A&B TV limited. All rights reserved. Roobarb & Custard created by Grange Calveley.

© Mogzilla 2010 www.mogzilla.co.uk/roobarbandcustard ISBN: 978-1-906132-14-9 Printed in Malta. 5 4 3 2 1

It was early in the morning and Roobarb was hard at work
m e a s u r i n g,
hammering
and smoothing things down.

'What on earth are you doing?' asked Custard,
sliding off his fence to get a closer look.

'I'm getting rid of all the bumps, and making everything smooth!'

'Don't you mean 'rough', as you dogs say?' sniggered Custard.

And with that, he strutted off to the shed, followed by Mouse who was carrying a fur-drier.

'That smooth-talking old dog,'

Custard grumbled, slipping over to Moggy Malone and Poodle Princess as they prepared for their tea-time dance show.

'Custard, m'dear, can you pass me the fur-drier?' asked Moggy.
'I can't. Roobarb's got it in the shed,' muttered Custard.

Without warning, a siren blared and a voice announced:

'PLEASE STAND BACK!
TESTING FOR ROOBARB'S LATEST INVENTION
IS ABOUT TO BEGIN!'

Roobarb's new invention was powered by the puff from Moggy's fur-drier.

Everyone watched, amazed, as he glided across the garden.

Mouse gave his guitar a Spanish strum, and Roobarb began his Flamenco dance through the air.

All the animals gathered round, and gawped at Roobarb's glorious machine.

Walking was clearly a thing of the past!

Poodle Princess joined in the dance, her paws held high, as the music played faster and faster.

With all the excitement, Roobarb felt like he was flying...

and then he was!

The fur-drier's controls hit full power, catapulting him into the sky.

Roobarb rose upwards, over the tops of trees and clouds. His fans roared with excitement, until...

With a terrible

C R A S H !!!

The show was

over.

'I'm in another world,' thought Roobarb,

'I landed perfectly!

Everyone loves my new invention!'

And he presented a crushed rose to Poodle Princess.

'Oh, Roobarb, darling!' she cooed.

As Roobarb fainted into Poodle Princess' arms, the shed door flew open.

'Look, everyone! It's amazing!

I think I've perfected...
the Hover-Shed!'
cried Mouse.

More marvellous adventures with Roobarb & Custard!

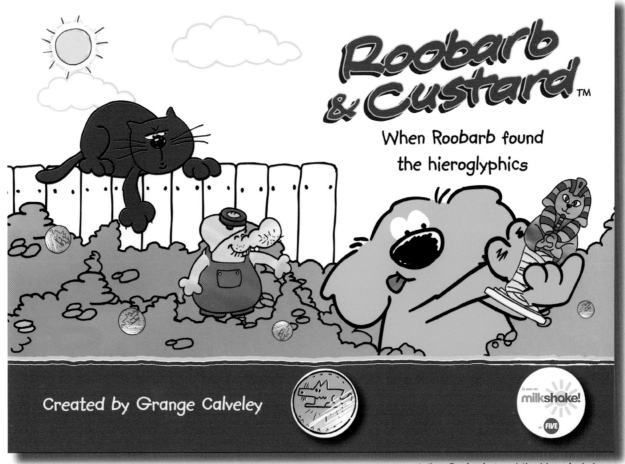

Roobarb & Custard™

When Roobarb found the hieroglyphics

Created by Grange Calveley

When Roobarb found the hieroglyphsics
ISBN: 978-1-906132-11-8

Bag yourself more Roobarb & Custard books online at

www.mogzilla.co.uk/shop

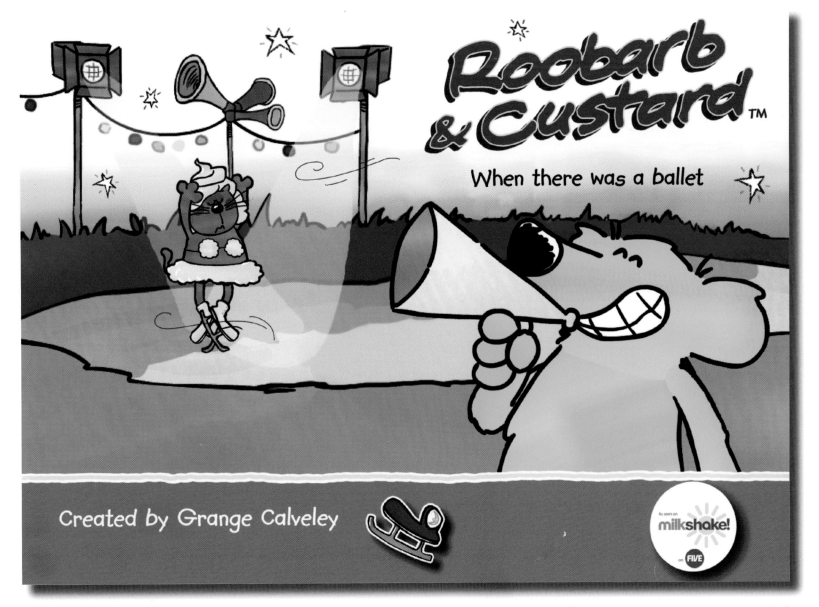

Roobarb & Custard™

When there was a ballet

Created by Grange Calveley

As seen on milkshake! on FIVE

When there was a ballet
ISBN: 978-1-906132-13-2

Roobarb & Custard™

When Custard was grounded

Created by Grange Calveley

When Custard was grounded
ISBN: 978-1-906132-10-1